Adapted by Carol Greene

Illustrations by The Krislin Company
Frank Rocco, Illustrator

Based on *Die Roten Stiefel* by Dr. Paul Chrystoph and the Teleplay
Red Boots for Christmas by Sheryl Scarborough and Kayte Kuch
for Lutheran Hour Ministries

Partial funding for the publication of this book has been provided by a grant from
Aid Association for Lutherans, Appleton, Wisconsin.

Published by Concordia Publishing House
3558 S. Jefferson Avenue, St. Louis, MO 63118-3968

Manufactured in Mexico

1 2 3 4 5 6 7 8 9 10   04 03 02 01 00 99 98 97 96 95

Soft snow fell on the village of Friedensdorf, but the village lights glowed warm, and so did the hearts of the villagers as they made ready for Christmas.

$\mathcal{P}$astor put up the Nativity scene in front of the church. In other parts of the village, Brigetta the paperseller waved a special Christmas edition of the newspaper. Karla the candlemaker hung decorations outside her shop, and Frederick the mailman delivered Christmas cards.

Spoiled young Adelaide whined and pulled at her father. He was mayor of Friedensdorf, a rich, important man, and he'd promised to buy her the finest Christmas present in the village.

*O*nly Hans the shoemaker was grumpy and gloomy.

"Christmas is just another excuse to be greedy," he told Aldo, his pet crow. "And I won't be a part of it."

Then Gretchen the woodgatherer came to Hans' shop and showed him a shabby old pair of shoes. "Will you fix these?" she asked. "They're my Christmas present to my granddaughter Elsa. Her little feet get so cold. I can pay you with this fine bundle of twigs."

"It would take a miracle to fix those shoes!" said Hans. "And twigs won't buy my supper. Everyone is so worried about Christmas gifts!"

"*H*ans," said Gretchen, "Christmas gifts are a symbol of God's great gift to us—His Son, Jesus Christ, born in Bethlehem to be Savior of the world."

But Hans didn't understand.

*T*hat night, as Hans was drifting off to sleep, a burst of light filled his room, and an angel spoke to him.

"I bring you good news," said the angel. "This Christmas you will receive a special gift, a gift from God."

$\mathcal{H}$ans couldn't believe his ears. A gift from God—to *HIM?*

*B*ut the next morning, Hans knew what he must do. If God had a gift for him, why, he must have one for God too—the finest gift in the village.

From shop to shop he went. At last he thought he'd found the gift—a music box filled with twirling Christmas trees.

$\mathcal{B}$ut young Adelaide wanted it too, and her father had more money than Hans. So off Hans trudged to look some more.

Out in the street Hans met Gretchen and Elsa. "Gretchen," he asked, "what would *you* give God for Christmas?"

"Well," said Gretchen, "I would give Him what I give Him every day—my sins for His pardon, my weakness for His strength, and my sorrow for His joy."

ℋans didn't understand that at all. But then he looked at little Elsa. She was stuffing her worn-out shoes with paper to help keep out the cold. And that gave Hans an idea.

Hans hurried home, locked himself in his shop, and began to gather some things together. As he worked, he sang. He did not sing well.

"It's been too long since I've sung a Christmas song," he told Aldo. "But look, I've saved this red leather for a long time. It's the finest in the land. Here are silver nails, handmade by my father. And these silver bells are from my first Christmas tree. I'm making a gift, Aldo! A Christmas gift."

$\mathcal{H}$ans worked all night and into the next morning. "They're done, Aldo!" he said at last. Aldo whistled. There sat a pair of tiny red boots, beautiful boots, magnificent enough for a king.

ans put the boots in the window where everyone could see them. But he wouldn't sell them, not even to the mayor for young Adelaide. Those boots were Hans' gift to God.

$\mathcal{H}$ans spent the afternoon cooking a fine dinner. Soon it would be Christmas Eve, and God would visit him with the special gift. Hans thought God would like a fine dinner too.

*A*s Hans worked, he sang some more. He sounded better now.

But Christmas Eve came, and the only people who knocked at Hans' door were Frederick the mailman, Brigetta the paperseller, and the mayor. So Hans served his dinner to them. And before they ate, he sang a song, a Christmas song he remembered from his childhood.

"*From heaven above to earth I come
To bring good news to everyone.
Glad tidings of great joy I bring
To all the world and gladly sing ...*"

Hans sang it very well.

*A*fter dinner, Hans' guests left. It had been a lovely evening, but Hans felt sad. Then lights filled the room, and the angel appeared again.

"Oh, it's you," said Hans. "I had everything ready. But I did not get my special gift from God."

"Let me help you understand, Hans," said the angel. "Look at that Nativity scene. Giving Christmas gifts is a fine custom. But the real message of Christmas is God's gift of His Son. 'For unto you is born this day … a Savior, which is Christ the Lord.'"

25

$\mathcal{T}$he angel left and, all at once, Hans *did* understand.

" 'A Savior, which is Christ the Lord!' *That* is the real gift, for me and for everyone!"

$\mathcal{T}$hen a moonbeam touched the red boots, and Hans understood something else. He grabbed the boots and ran outside. All the villagers were on their way to midnight worship, but Hans hurried straight to Elsa.

"Here, child," he said. "A Christmas present." And he put the red boots on her cold little feet.

$\mathcal{N}$earby stood the mayor and young Adelaide. Adelaide wanted those boots very much, and she began to whine.

"Hush, child," said her father. "This is what Christmas is all about. We give to each other because God has given us the greatest gift of all."

For a moment Adelaide was quiet, and in that moment she understood too. So she gave Elsa another gift, the music box filled with twirling Christmas trees.

*T*hen, as the soft snow sifted down and the church lights glowed, the village of Friedensdorf sang the great glad news of Christmas.

"*To you this night is born a Child,*
Of Mary, chosen virgin mild.
This newborn Child of lowly birth
Shall be the joy of all the earth."

*A*nd from the heavens echoed an angel voice: "For unto you is born this day in the city of David a Savior, which is Christ the Lord."